ANIMAL JAM ®

THE PHANTOMS' SECRET

BY CHRISTA ROBERTS

Penguin Young Readers Licenses
An Imprint of Penguin Random House

PENGUIN YOUNG READERS LICENSES
An Imprint of Penguin Random House LLC

Cover illustrated by Jemma Kemker

ISBN 9780451534484   10 9 8 7 6 5 4 3 2 1

CHAPTER ONE

"This is even better than I thought it would be!" Peck said, her purple bunny ears twitching with excitement.

"I know!" Katie the deer said, walking over to join Peck at the dessert table. "It's my first bonfire! I'm so excited!"

Night was beginning to fall in Sarepia Forest, and the party of the year was just getting started. The normally quiet forest was abuzz with activity. Raccoons danced the cha-cha and clapped while a polar bear wearing a sparkly vest beat a hand drum.

Toucans swooped down with fragrant flower wreaths, dropping them on the heads of delighted foxes and deer. Penguins were struggling to carry platters of sandwiches and fruit kebabs to tables that were already filled with food. And in the center of it all, a giant bonfire blazed and crackled.

"It looks like a painting!" Peck clasped her paws together. "I want to freeze this in my mind forever!" Tonight was one of the most special events of the year—the annual Jamaa bonfire to celebrate the summer solstice, the day when the sun would reach its highest peak in the sky. The solstice was two days away, and the animals of Jamaa had been planning the festivities for weeks. As one of the six Alphas, Peck had been responsible for arranging the music and decorations.

"You don't have to worry about remembering it." Katie popped a chocolate chip cookie into her mouth. "Just ask Liza for a picture. She's been taking them all night."

"Oh!" Peck replied. "That reminds me, I need to ask her about something." Peck looked around and spotted Graham, the inquisitive monkey Alpha, adjusting a string of lights in the trees. Nearby at the bonfire, Sir Gilbert, the regal tiger Alpha, was getting ready to tell a story. And not too far off, sure enough, there was Liza! The friendly panda Alpha was snapping photos of a group of energetic animals with garlands of brightly colored orchids around their necks.

Peck waved goodbye to Katie and zoomed through the crowd, weaving in and out between the dancing and singing animals.

"Okay, everyone. If the giraffes can just stand in the back and let the pigs scoot up front, that's going to be absolutely perfect." Liza was holding up her lens to frame the shot. "And there's still enough light for me to shoot without using my flash."

"Liza! Hey!" Peck skidded to a stop next to the panda Alpha's side. "I've got to talk to you. It's, um, kind of urgent." She shot an apologetic glance over at the pigs. "Sorry to interrupt the moment, guys."

Click. Liza took a quick picture and put her camera down. "What's the matter, Peck? Is everything okay?" Her dark eyes filled with concern. "If you're worried about the party, it looks like everyone is having a blast."

Peck shook her head quickly. "No, no, that's not it. I need to tell you something.

Privately." She took Liza's arm and ushered her away from the curious crowd.

Peck's voice was low. "I went over to Bunny Burrow earlier today to make sure everybody knew what time the festivities were starting tonight." She took a gulp of air. "But nobody was in a party mood. The fields where the bunnies grow all the vegetables? Zilch. Zippo. Nothing."

Liza frowned. "I don't understand."

"Me either," Peck said. "The bunnies planted the usual—carrots, lettuce, broccoli, peppers—but no luck. All the plants are wilting and dying!"

"Hmmm. Are the plants getting enough water?" Liza asked. "It has been very warm lately—and we're only two days away from the solstice."

Peck nodded impatiently. "The head

farmer told me the bunnies have been watering twice a day and fertilizing, just like always. Something's not right." Out of the corner of her eye, Liza noticed Cosmo walking by. She waved him over. "Hey, Cosmo, come here!" Cosmo was the koala Alpha—and an expert on plants.

Cosmo ambled over to his Alpha friends, balancing a plate of cheese and crackers in one paw and holding his ever-present wooden staff in the other. He listened closely as the bunny Alpha repeated her story. "So that's it," Peck said breathlessly. "What do you think?"

The candle on top of Cosmo's staff flickered. "Hmm, that's very interesting. If you like, the three of us could go over to Bunny Burrow tomorrow and check it out," he told Peck and Liza. "Seeing the problem is the first step to solving the problem."

"That would be awesome!" Peck said, breaking out into a relieved smile.

"Thank you, Cosmo. If anyone can figure out what's going on with the bunnies' crops, it's you," Liza added.

Cosmo smiled. "Hot windy days can cause havoc with some plants. And if the bunnies are overwatering, soil drainage could be an issue. We'll sort it out." He bopped his head to the distant drumbeat and headed off toward the party. "Now if you'll excuse me, I've got a solstice to celebrate!"

Hot summer sun? Dry winds? Peck hoped that was all it was. Because what she hadn't said aloud—what she'd been afraid to even think—was that the problem with the bunnies' crops was far more worrisome than something a little water—or lack thereof—could solve.

"Gather round, gather round." Sir Gilbert's deep voice boomed across the bonfire. A group of younger animals had assembled around the large orange tiger, perched on logs and tree stumps, transfixed by his commanding presence. "On an occasion such as this, on an evening such as this, it is important for us to remember where we came from, and how our beautiful Jamaa was once almost lost forever."

A shiver of excitement went through the crowd. Everyone was up for a good story. And Sir Gilbert was one of the best storytellers in all of Jamaa.

"It was a dark period in our world's past," Sir Gilbert said quietly. "Animals had stopped trusting one another. Friends became enemies. Communities grew divided. Communication broke down. Species took their Heartstones—the special jewels that held the essence and secrets of each species given to them by Mira and Zios, the guardian spirits of Jamaa—and hid them away. And it was then, during this time of division and fear, that the dark Phantoms first appeared."

"I'm scared," whispered a little sloth, burying his face in his sloth friend's shoulder.

"As you should be," Sir Gilbert admonished. "Wherever the Phantoms went, destruction followed. They destroyed villages and corrupted our land. They began to capture the Heartstones, and with that, entire species disappeared from Jamaa. Soon there were only six species left: monkeys, koalas, pandas, bunnies, wolves, and—"

"Tigers!" a young tiger piped up eagerly. "Tell us about the battles, Sir Gilbert!" the cub pleaded. "Did you come face-to-face with the Phantom Queen?"

Sir Gilbert held up his paw, his metal cuff glinting in the firelight. "All in good time, young sir. All in good time. Now, Mira and Zios saw that in order to save Jamaa, they would need to find leaders of these species to come together to battle the Phantoms. And that is when Graham, Cosmo, Liza, Peck, Greely, and myself were chosen as the Alphas. Mira and Zios entrusted the Alpha Stones to our care and gave us a charge to unite Jamaa in its darkest hour and to help save the land!"

The regal tiger held his chin high as

the animals stopped eating, hanging on his every word. "The battle was epic. For we were fighting not just for ourselves, but for the promise of what Jamaa had been and could be once again. Every animal in Jamaa joined our crusade, and victory was in sight as the cowardly Phantoms fled into their dark portals. Yet just as the last of the Phantoms were retreating, the Phantom Queen overtook Zios and vanished with him into a portal. The courageous Mira dove in after them. And it was then"—Sir Gilbert paused, his voice heavy with emotion—"that Mira called out to me, bequeathing upon me the important mission of finding her."

The animals bowed their heads. For although many years had passed since the great battle Sir Gilbert spoke of, Mira and

Zios were still out there, missing.

When Sir Gilbert finished his speech, he inspected the dessert table. Young animals followed him and peppered him with questions. As the tiger Alpha took a bite of cake and started to expound on details of the battle, he noticed Greely, the mysterious wolf Alpha, standing by himself in the shadows. A couple of chattering foxes walked by, startling when they realized Greely was there. The foxes scurried off. No one ever wanted to be in Greely's way.

"Excuse me," Sir Gilbert said to the animals. Then he walked over to Greely. "Have you tried the chocolate cake, Greely? It's simply delicious."

Greely didn't respond. Instead, he looked out at the party, studying it.

"Now, you know, Greely, this is a party," Sir Gilbert chided. "If you tried to mingle, you might actually surprise yourself and have a little fun."

Again, silence.

Sir Gilbert sighed. "Obviously you're having quite a good time standing over here by yourself in the dark. How are the shadows treating you? Any nefarious deeds I should be aware of?"

Greely remained silent, but something in his expression shifted.

Sir Gilbert studied him. "If there is something wrong, Greely, you should share it. Mira and Zios always wanted us to work together as a team."

Greely turned to him, his yellow eyes glowing and calculating. The mention of the guardian spirits' names had the effect on the wolf that Sir Gilbert had hoped for. "There may be something . . . " the wolf said slowly, finally breaking the silence. "One of my sources saw something strange appear in Coral Canyons."

"Something strange? What was it?" Sir Gilbert asked, meeting Greely's gaze. The two Alphas began to walk deeper into the woods for privacy. "And is your source a reliable one?"

"Ivan the eagle. He said he saw a large crystal clear pool there," Greely answered, his voice void of any emotion. His dark purple cloak rippled in the night breeze.

A look of confusion furrowed Sir Gilbert's brow. "A crystal clear pool? In Coral Canyons?" Sir Gilbert repeated. "Well that doesn't make much sense."

Coral Canyons was a place of rocky

trails and red rock mesas. It was a beautiful land, but it was a desert. Everyone knew where to find the occasional stream, but if Ivan the eagle had seen an undiscovered pool there, it was something strange, indeed.

"And there's something else," Greely said, his narrow-set eyes shifting in the dark. "Ivan said there was a statue in the middle of the pool . . . a statue with a remarkable resemblance to Mira."

Sir Gilbert rose on his haunches and came face-to-face with Greely. "A statue shaped like Mira? We must go there at once!" His excitement was palpable. "This may be the sign I've been looking for. The sign that can bring Mira home at last!"

Greely was silent for a moment, appearing to weigh the tiger's words over.

"I will speak with Ivan and gather more information."

"*We* will speak with Ivan," Sir Gilbert corrected, feeling a flicker of annoyance at Greely's stubborn independence. "You know as well as I that we need to work together if we want to succeed."

Greely's eyes narrowed, his white tufted eyebrows forming a V.

"Greely—" the tiger started, but before he could finish, Greely held up a paw.

"We leave tomorrow." He sighed. "At sunrise." And without another word, the mysterious gray wolf vanished into the night.

CHAPTER TWO

Last night's bonfire was a smoldering pile of ash by the time Sir Gilbert woke up. After the festivities were over, the Alphas had decided they would all sleep at Alphas Hollow. The Hollow was a secluded spot, hidden inside a massive tree—a place that not even the animals of Jamaa knew about. It was here that the Alphas could talk freely and work together to keep Jamaa safe.

Sir Gilbert yawned, blinking in the predawn light, and stretched on the cushion he'd slept on. Maybe he would have something to eat, or possibly a cup of hot tea, before he set out. He looked at the corner where Greely usually slept, but the wolf wasn't there. Instead, Greely was already waiting for him by the door.

"You slept late," Greely remarked before turning to walk outside. Sir Gilbert followed and was startled when the wolf lifted up his head and let out a long, wailing howl. The sound echoed through the trees and across the mountaintops of Jamaa.

They had planned to meet at sunrise and the sun hadn't risen yet, but Sir Gilbert decided not to correct Greely. "Good morning to you as well," Sir Gilbert said, his tone brusque. There was no point wasting time arguing.

Sir Gilbert knew that the howl was more than just a morning ritual for the wolf Alpha—it acted as a signal to other animals. Sure enough, Sir Gilbert soon heard the sound of wings flapping. A majestic eagle appeared in the bright blue sky above them. Ivan's powerful wing beats had him gliding onto the ground in front of the Alphas in seconds.

"Greely. Sir Gilbert." Ivan nodded respectfully.

"Greetings," Sir Gilbert said, nodding back. "Beautiful morning for a flight. Fascinating how you—"

"Ivan, please share with us what you saw the other day," Greely interrupted, getting straight to the point.

"Ah, yes." Sir Gilbert straightened his spine and looked at the eagle attentively.

The eagle's golden eyes blinked. "I was out on a morning flight a few days ago—the sun was out, and I was able to catch a warm, rising current. I let it take me over Jamaa and to the outskirts of Coral Canyons. It's one of my favorite places to fly."

"And what did you see there?" Greely asked, sitting back on his haunches.

Ivan continued. "The usual. Rocky trails and the red rock mesas. All the things that I normally see when I fly over the desert. But then, I saw something very strange. I saw . . . a pool."

"A pool?" Sir Gilbert repeated. "Are you sure?"

Ivan nodded his head. "An eagle's eyes never lie. It was a perfectly round blue pool of water, sitting in the middle of Coral Canyons." He looked from Sir Gilbert to Greely. "And what was even stranger was that there was a statue of

Mira in the middle of the pool."

"But how can you be sure?" Sir Gilbert demanded. Greely had told him all this the night before, but now that Sir Gilbert was hearing it from the source, he grew anxious.

"An eagle's vision is one of his strongest traits," Greely cut him off. "If Ivan says it was a statue of Mira, then that's what it was."

Sir Gilbert paced back and forth, his claws digging into the dewy morning grass. "There is no doubt, then. This is a sign from Mira. She is trying to tell us something. We have to figure out what it is." He wanted Greely to agree with him, but as usual, the wolf Alpha was impossible to read—his expression revealed nothing and his rigid stance betrayed no emotion.

"Coral Canyons is a gigantic place," Ivan

said. "If you like, I can take you to where I saw the pool."

"Yes. We must go. Right, Greely?" But when Sir Gilbert turned to him for confirmation, he was surprised to see that he was alone. Greely was already walking down the path toward the desert.

"There's no time to waste." Greely's voice cut back through the forest. "If Mira is sending us a message, we need to find out what it is."

"I didn't sleep very well last night," Peck confessed later that morning as she, Cosmo, and Liza walked through Sarepia Forest on their way to Bunny Burrow. She and Cosmo were doing their best to keep up with Liza's long strides. The air was cool and crisp; birds chirped happily from their nest above, and sunlight filtered through the giant trees. "I couldn't stop thinking about the crops."

"Me too," admitted Liza, stepping over a fallen branch. "What do you think's going on, Cosmo?"

The thoughtful koala Alpha had stopped next to a large flowering bush. He tilted his head, as if he was listening to someone speak. "That's very interesting," he murmured to himself, nodding. Then he caught up to Peck and Liza. "This part of the forest has had plenty of sunshine and rain."

"Which makes the bunnies' problem a mystery," Peck said, her paws on her hips.

When the Alphas arrived at Bunny Burrow, a group of bunnies hurried out from their dens to greet them. "We're so glad you're here. We're really worried," a bunny with tiny front teeth said anxiously. "Please, follow us." The group went straight to the fields. There were hundreds of rows of plants . . . and all of them were dying. The carrot leaves were covered with spots. Rows of lettuce were wilted and yellow. And the cucumber vines were withered.

"I've been planting vegetables for years and I've never seen anything like this," said a tall bunny named Joe. He snapped a sad-looking cucumber off the vine and held it up. "We didn't want to jump to any conclusions . . . but there's been some talk if, maybe, the Phantoms are behind this?"

Everyone exchanged uneasy glances. Joe had said exactly what Peck had been thinking. It had taken years to restore all of the destruction the Phantoms had caused when they first came to Jamaa. If they were behind the dying crops, that could mean they were trying to once again claim Jamaa as their own.

"It could be many things. Let me see what I can find out," Cosmo said, reassuringly. Then he walked down a narrow dirt path filled with tomato plants and crouched down to their level.

"What's he doing?" a bunny named Maria asked, trying to get a better look.

"Plants tell him things," Peck explained, feeling a rush of hope that maybe Cosmo would be able to solve the problem. She hopped down the row to join him, the worried bunnies following her. The tomato plants were drooping, and rotten tomatoes covered the ground.

Cosmo carefully lifted a sick-looking

branch and held it up to his ear, whispering softly. The bunnies looked from Cosmo to the plants and then back at Cosmo again. "What is he—"

"Shhh!" Peck said, putting her paw to her mouth. "Wait."

A few seconds later, Cosmo gently put the plant back down on the ground and stood up, looking concerned. "The tomatoes are so weak that it's hard to hear them, but from what I gathered, there seems to be something wrong with their water."

"Are they not getting enough?" Liza wondered.

The bunnies all shook their heads. "We've had a lot of rain and we make sure to water the plants, too," Maria said as the other bunnies nodded.

Cosmo tapped his chin. "No . . . they're

getting enough . . . but there's something wrong with it." He bent down to listen again. "Something, erm, dangerous."

"Like poison?" Peck wondered aloud. The bunnies covered their mouths in alarm.

"Tough to say. Could be some type of virus or bacteria," Cosmo answered. "Whatever it is, it's hurting the plants."

"Does that mean they're going to die?" Liza asked, her eyes wide with concern.

Cosmo looked grim. "If we don't figure out what it is, yes. And if the water's polluted, it's not just bad for the plants, it's devastating for all of Jamaa. The streams flow into the waters of Crystal Sands—"

"And that's the water that flows into the ocean," Peck finished, the urgency of the situation clear.

"So if there's a problem here, there

could be a much bigger problem for all of us," Liza said solemnly. The bunnies looked at one another, frightened.

Peck's mind was spinning. "But before we jump to conclusions, we need to be absolutely sure the water is polluted."

Cosmo nodded. "We should test it."

"But how are you going to do that?" Joe the bunny asked, pulling worriedly on his whiskers.

Peck's face brightened. "Meet me at the stream. I'm going to find Graham," she exclaimed. The monkey Alpha had zillions of inventions.

"Great idea, Peck," Liza said. "If anyone has a gizmo to find out if our water is polluted or not, it's Graham!"

CHAPTER THREE

The sun was high overhead when Sir Gilbert
and Greely reached Coral Canyons. The
temperature was sweltering, but Greely
barely noticed. His eyes were busy scanning
the surrounding desert for Phantoms. He
stared up at the massive red sandstone cliffs
that towered over them, but other than the
sound of a small creature scampering under
a rock, there was nothing but silence.

"This is the place?" he called to Ivan.
The giant eagle hovered in the air above
the Alphas.

"Almost. Just past these boulders," Ivan said, flying several yards ahead.

When Sir Gilbert and Greely rounded the curve, they came to a stop. It was just as Ivan had told them. There, in the middle of the desert, stood a pool of the most brilliant blue water. The surface was as smooth and flat as a mirror. And in the middle of the pool was a blue-gray marble statue of Mira. Her broad round wings were spread wide and her long, elegant neck was curved downward. She was standing on her right foot, her left foot raised slightly. The statue had captured her poise and elegance perfectly.

"The statue. The pool. It is real," Sir Gilbert whispered, the fur on his neck bristling. He and Greely walked to the edge of the water.

"And now, if you'll excuse me, I must

be off," Ivan said with a slight bow. "I hope you find what you're looking for." The eagle glided up into the sky. In seconds, he was out of sight.

A warm wind blew through the canyon, ruffling Greely's and Sir Gilbert's fur. They stared at the statue of Mira. Suddenly, the marble began to glow, and the still water of the pool shimmered. Ripples fluttered across the surface. Water began to jet out of a spout in her neck in a high, graceful arc. It appeared that the statue was actually a fountain.

"Look," Sir Gilbert said as a rainbow burst across the brilliant blue sky.

Now Greely was the one who looked like a statue. He stood motionless. Waiting. Watching. Ready.

And then, out of nowhere, came a

sound the Alphas had waited forever to hear once more. "Greely. Sir Gilbert. It is so good to see you." Mira's ethereal voice surrounded them. It seemed to come from around them, bouncing off the cliffs and rocks.

"Mira!" Sir Gilbert exclaimed, gazing at the rainbow. "Is it really you? It's been so long!" He straightened his posture and bowed his head. "We have missed you so very much."

"Know that I am always with you," Mira said kindly. "But now, I need your help."

A feeling of calmness settled over Greely at the sound of Mira's voice. He focused intently on the glowing statue. "What do you need us to do?" he asked.

"Tomorrow is the summer solstice. The sun will be at its highest point," Mira said.

"And this year, unlike in years past, the planets have perfectly aligned. Because of that, there may be a way for me to come back to Jamaa."

Sir Gilbert couldn't believe what he was hearing. He gazed over at Greely in disbelief but the wolf's full attention was on the statue. "How?" Sir Gilbert asked.

Mira's voice was clear and calm. "There are three things that represent the land of Jamaa, the land of rivers and forests and oceans that you have served and protected so well all these years. If you can collect these three things and bring them back to this fountain, I may be able to create a portal to come back to Jamaa."

"Wait, are you safe? Where are you? Is Zios with you?" Sir Gilbert asked. No one had seen Mira or Zios since the day the guardian spirits had disappeared into the Phantoms' portal.

"We are in a place of dark power," Mira answered. Sir Gilbert could feel the sadness in her voice. "It is a place where the Phantoms run wild, acting out their horrible vision for the world. And while we have battled great evil and witnessed terrible crimes, please know that we are as safe as we can be, considering the circumstances. Zios and I have battled hard against the Phantoms and their wickedness. Knowing that we had left you in Jamaa to carry on the battle there is what has kept us going."

"So Zios is still alive?" Greely asked, his body taut.

"Yes," Mira said. "But we decided to separate to try and find a way back to Jamaa. Only one of us can attempt to make the journey, and we have agreed it will be me."

"Tell us what we need to find, Mira," Greely said, and for once Sir Gilbert was glad to get right to the point.

"We will start collecting right away and have you back in Jamaa before night falls," Sir Gilbert promised Mira, willing it to be true.

The rainbow's colors faded and then began to deepen in color again. "I'm afraid it won't be that easy," Mira said, her tone cautionary. "The dark power here works like a curtain of deception. It prevents me from being able to tell you what the objects are."

"Then how will we know what they are?" Sir Gilbert said, dismayed.

Greely's face darkened. "What can you tell us?"

"You must use your extraordinary skills to solve the mystery of three riddles," Mira said, not directly answering their questions. "The answer to each riddle will tell you the name of one of the objects. And there is one more thing," Mira continued. "This is of the utmost importance. Once the sun is highest in the sky, signifying the solstice, you will need to activate the objects by focusing and harnessing your natural powers."

Sir Gilbert looked up at the golden sun above and back to the shimmering fountain. "Of course, Mira. What are the riddles?" Sir Gilbert asked. His ears swiveled upward as he focused on Mira's words.

"The first riddle is this," Mira said.

I am admired for my beauty.
No one else is like me.

Only some can make me.

And everyone wants to take me."

The water in the fountain rippled and then smoothed. The guardian spirit continued. "The second riddle is this:

I hang from the sky

and lie on the ground.

I am closed or open,

long or small."

The two Alphas listened carefully to Mira's words, committing the riddles to memory. "And the last riddle for you is this." Mira's voice rang out loud and clear.

"Sometimes I'm fast,

and sometimes I'm slow.

I always fall but won't stand up,

I'm free for all but can't be bought."

"The solstice will be here in less than twenty-four hours," Greely said. "If the riddles are solved before then, is your return guaranteed?"

"I wish for that to be so, but unfortunately, there are no guarantees," Mira said. Her voice was thick with emotion. "But if there ever is a moment where I might be able to return to you and to Jamaa, this is it. I wish you the best of luck in your search." Suddenly the marble statue was emblazoned with light. And then, just as quickly, the light was sucked away. The water in the pool shimmered and then returned to complete stillness. The warm wind that had blown through the canyon was replaced with a quick, cool breeze.

And in the silence, it was as if Mira had never been there at all.

The enormity of the moment hung in the air between the Alphas. If they could solve the riddles, Mira might be able to be with them once again! The significance of the guardian spirits was hard to put into words. It was the guardian spirits who had given each species a Heartstone. And when Jamaa was on the verge of destruction, it was the guardian spirits who had found the six animal leaders. Having Mira and Zios back in Jamaa, living among them, protecting them, and teaching them had been the Alphas' biggest wish.

"This is the best chance we've had since the great battle to get Mira back," Sir Gilbert said. "Everyone is counting on us . . . we cannot let Mira down." It felt like he had been waiting his entire life for this singular moment. He lifted his head proudly.

"You give yourself too much credit,

Sir Gilbert," Greely said in a scornful voice. "No one even knows about this. But it doesn't matter," he continued, seeing Sir Gilbert's hurt look. "We will not let her down." His steely eyes glinted with determination.

The wolf Alpha lifted his face toward the sky, and Sir Gilbert joined him. Together, the two Alphas looked up at the sun. "The clock is ticking," Sir Gilbert said as they turned and raced back in the direction they had come. "There is no time to waste. It is time to solve the riddles!"

CHAPTER FOUR

Back at Bunny Burrow, Peck left Cosmo, Liza, and the bunnies and flew through the woods back to Alphas Hollow. She knew it was a safe bet that Graham could be found at his workshop: a large shed with a table pushed against the wall that contained all the bits and pieces of the monkey's latest projects. A smoothie machine that picked, washed, and blended fruit. A contraption that washed your face and dried your paws all at once. A mechanical hand that could reach the highest bunches of bananas in the trees. Graham had a lot of projects.

Sure enough, he was at his table now with what looked like a salad spinner: a clear bowl, a strainer that fit inside, and a lid with little tabs.

"Now, if I snap the lid on like this," Graham muttered to himself, putting the lid on top of the bowl, "these tabs should lock into place like this." He peered through his goggles and pushed down on the tabs and they locked into place. "And then the top should rotate, but it's not working." He unsnapped the tabs, then snapped them again.

"Graham!" Peck cried, waving her paws to grab his attention. "We need your help!"

"You need me to make a salad for you?" Graham asked, trying unsuccessfully to get the spinner to turn. "Or wash your socks?

My spin-sock-salader does it all."

"Sounds cool, but not now," Peck said, catching her breath. "I raced all the way here to get you."

But Graham was distracted. "I left this thingamajig out in the sun to dry and it hasn't worked right ever since," he said, scratching his head. "There was also that pair of socks that got stuck. Maybe I should just stick to lettuce."

Peck blew out her breath. "Graham, if you don't help me, there won't be any lettuce for you to put in that thing." Now she had his attention. After she explained the problem at Bunny Burrow, Graham quickly tossed a backpack together filled with his tools and gadgets. Balls of twine, a tiny hammer, paper clips, a wrench, sandpaper—Graham had it all. He handed

Peck a small white cooler, and together, the two Alphas zipped back to meet Cosmo and Liza at the stream.

The bunnies' water source was at the top of a high mountain. Trees dotted the cliffs, and grass as high as Peck's waist waved in the soft breeze as they hiked up. When they got to the top, they quickly spotted Liza and Cosmo waiting for them in a small clearing. A thick canopy of leaves kept the sunlight out. The air was cool.

"We tried to get back here as fast as possible," Peck told them, blowing back the fur that covered her eye.

Graham tapped his bearded white chin and grinned. "Well, technically, if we were trying to get here as fast as possible, we would have used vines to swing from tree to tree," he pointed out. "If only the jet packs I made last month actually worked."

Peck would have giggled if it hadn't been such a serious situation. She bit her tongue and watched as Graham shook out the contents of his backpack onto the ground. Everything landed in a jumbled heap. That was probably what Graham's brain was like—a lot of cool stuff all mixed together.

"Liza and I thought this would be the best location to test the water," Cosmo told them, gesturing around the clearing. His moss skirt rustled. "Not many animals come here. Our findings will be uncontaminated."

"While we waited for you I took photos of some of the rapids and waterfalls," Liza told them, holding up her camera. "In case we want to look at them later."

"That's smart," Peck said, nodding as Graham rifled through his pack. He was mumbling something about "sterile technique" and "bad counts."

"Ideally we'd have a more controlled setting, but we're just going to have to improvise," Graham said, sounding resigned. "I tried to bring as many tools as I could."

"And we even brought a cooler," Peck said, putting a small white chest filled with ice on the ground. She was hopping around with nervous energy. "I'm not sure why!"

Graham held up a small black kit that was on the ground and unzipped it. Inside were four test tubes held in place by elastic bands. "I need you each to go to a different spot along the water's edge," he said. He carefully took the test tubes out and handed one to each of the Alphas. Next, he passed out small cork stoppers. "Fill your tube almost to the top with water and then put the stopper inside it and bring it back." He shook his head, mumbling to himself. "If we had more time, I'd run more tests, but this will have to do."

The Alphas found different spots in the stream and swiftly did as Graham asked. Then they regrouped next to Graham. He had set up an informal lab in the middle of the clearing with a small red blanket spread out on the ground and the cooler on top, its lid removed.

"Now what?" Peck asked excitedly. She pushed the stopper onto her tube with her paw. "It's weird to think that this water might be polluted. It's so clear!"

"That's why we have to test it," Graham

said, squinting through his goggles. "Looks can be deceiving." The monkey Alpha stood the tubes up in a small rack fashioned out of twigs and put the rack into the cooler. "The ice is going to prevent bacteria from growing in the tube. Bacteria reproduces very quickly," he pointed out. "Now we need to label the tubes with the date and time. Who has the neatest handwriting?"

"Liza," Cosmo said, passing her a pen. Liza carefully wrote the date and time on each tube.

Graham reached in his backpack and pulled out a bunch of long, thin green leaves. "I've created a special pollution test," he said. "Each of these leaves has a cluster of water-safe chemicals on the tip. If the water is polluted, the leaves will turn bright magenta."

"And what if the water isn't polluted?" Peck asked.

"Why, nothing at all! The leaves stay green," Graham said as he put a leaf inside each tube. In seconds, the Alphas had their answer.

Every leaf had turned purple.

"The leaves are the same color as me!" Peck cried, holding one up to her arm.

Cosmo held his head in his paws, looking pained. "We have our answer, then."

"There's no doubt about it," Graham said sadly. "The stream has been poisoned."

"And if Jamaa's water is poisoned, it's not only bad for the crops—it's bad for every living creature," Cosmo said solemnly.

The Alphas exchanged worried glances. They had known this was a possibility—but hearing Graham confirm their fears was not the outcome they had been hoping for.

"Do you need to run more tests?" Liza asked Graham. She snapped a few pictures of the purple-tipped leaves.

He scratched his head, thinking for a moment. "No more tests. But what I think we should do is track where the poison is coming from. This is a high elevation stream. We need to climb higher to find the source of the contamination."

Cosmo nodded. "That sounds like a good idea."

The Alphas gathered up all of Graham's things, making sure the test tubes were sealed and protected inside the cooler. Graham put the backpack on, and the other Alphas agreed to take turns carrying the cooler.

"It's so pretty up here," Peck said as

they made their way up the mountain, passing by a small cascade of water. "It would be nice to come up here for a picnic sometime." Then she sighed. "Can you imagine having a picnic next to this beautiful stream but not being able to drink the water? That would be awful!"

Liza nodded sympathetically and gave Peck a small pat on the shoulder while Cosmo and Graham trudged on.

A wind blew through the forest, making the leaves around them rustle. Cosmo motioned for the group to be quiet. "Shhh," he whispered, tilting his head upward. He listened intently for a moment. "I just heard a distress call. A group of pine trees are in danger up ahead," he said softly. "They're crying out for help. We must go to them now!"

The Alphas began running up the mountain, pushing past branches and sending rocks skittering.

"We're almost there!" Cosmo whispered loudly as they neared a large grove of trees. He held out his arm, making them all come to an abrupt stop. The clearing was filled with maples and junipers and pine trees, their trunks shaking and leaves and needles whirling everywhere. Flower petals were blown violently off their stems. The powerful smell of pine hung in the air.

"It's like a mini-tornado," Peck whispered, her eyes wide as Liza snapped some photos of the destruction.

Suddenly the grove lit up with a flash of blue-white light and the ground rumbled beneath their feet. "Something's burning," Graham murmured, and the strong smell of pine was replaced with the acrid scent of scorching wood.

"This isn't just some wacky weather—it's the Phantoms!" Cosmo exclaimed as another electric flash streaked across the sky.

The Alphas looked on helplessly as hundreds of Phantoms rampaged through the grove of trees. Some Phantoms were scaling the trees, sliding up and down the trunks, causing the bark to fall off. Others were shaking the trees wildly. There were Phantoms using rocks to make deep gouges in tree trunks. The oily creatures were hissing and snarling, delighting in the devastation they were causing.

"We can't just stand here and watch them destroy our world . . . we've got to do something!" Peck cried, her eyes blazing.

One of the Phantoms seemed to have heard Peck. He looked up at them from where he stood near a tall pine tree, his eye blinking rapidly. His tentacles whirled through the air so fast they looked almost bladelike. Then, without warning, he made a deep slice across the tree, causing it to shake. All the while, his cruel one-eyed gaze stayed focused on the Alphas, taunting them. Then he slipped away into the melee.

"Ohhhh!" Peck gasped, her paw flying to her mouth. Graham tightened his backpack onto his small shoulders, and Liza put down the cooler and adjusted her braid, a look of determination on both of their faces. Cosmo was white with rage.

"Let's do this," the koala gritted out. He gripped his staff, and together, the courageous Alphas raced forward into battle.

CHAPTER FIVE

"There is so much beauty in Jamaa it is hard to know where to start!" Sir Gilbert exclaimed, walking back and forth. He and Greely had stopped on the outskirts of Coral Canyons. For the past hour they'd been repeating the riddles to themselves, brainstorming on what the answers could be.

Or rather, Sir Gilbert was trying to brainstorm. Greely hadn't seemed all that interested in his ideas. And he wasn't sharing many thoughts of his own. Instead, he had climbed on top of a pile of smooth rocks and stared silently off into the distance.

"Now, let us go over this again," Sir Gilbert said. He repeated the riddle. "'I am admired for my beauty. No one else is like me. Only some can make me. And everyone wants to take me.' Sarepia Forest has a quiet beauty, dark with trees that touch the sky. And the beaches and clear waters of Crystal Sands are breathtaking. And Mt. Shiveer is beautiful if you like that kind of thing. Snow and ice and frozen tundra. I once went to—"

"The answer isn't a place," Greely cut in. "That would only make sense for the first part of the riddle. What about the second part?"

Sir Gilbert nodded. "True." He thought for a moment. "Maybe it is something to eat? Those chocolate chip cookies at the celebration the other night—everyone wanted to take those."

Greely rolled his eyes. "Are you saying a cookie represents the land of Jamaa?" He flicked an imaginary piece of dirt off his cloak. "You are wasting time."

Sir Gilbert sighed. "Apologies. You are right, of course. Sometimes thinking out loud helps me focus." Several minutes passed in silence. Sir Gilbert turned and looked back in the direction they'd come from. "But humor me for a moment. I am thinking back to Coral Canyons. There is a lovely shop located there, Epic Wonders. Have you ever been there, Greely?"

"Maybe," Greely said dismissively. He let out a low grumble. "What does a shop have to do with anything?"

Sir Gilbert continued, the wheels turning in his mind. "At Epic Wonders, they sell rare stones. I remember chatting with the shopkeeper there about her goods. We had a delightful little talk about a black opal that had recently come into her possession."

"A thrilling conversation, I'm sure," Greely said drily.

Sir Gilbert ignored him and went on. "She showed me one of her rarest items. A beautiful white pearl. Do you know how pearls are made, Greely? Fascinating process, really," Sir Gilbert paused for a second. "They are created by shelled mollusks."

Greely was paying attention now. "Beautiful. Rare. Made by a mollusk," he said slowly.

"And desirable," Sir Gilbert finished, his eyes shining. "A pearl. The answer to Mira's first riddle is a pearl!"

Greely nodded at Sir Gilbert, a smile almost forming. "Good job. We have our first answer. Now we need the pearl."

"The market for pearls is not robust, from what I can recall," Sir Gilbert said thoughtfully. He looked in the direction of Coral Canyons. "I daresay there's a good chance the shopkeeper hasn't sold—"

"But if she did sell it, we've wasted time by going there," Greely interrupted him. "Follow me." And before Sir Gilbert could respond, Greely took off running.

"Greely!" Sir Gilbert shouted. "Where are you off to? It is imperative that we make decisions together."

But the aloof wolf Alpha was already

too far ahead to hear him. "He has left me no choice," Sir Gilbert said with an aggravated sigh. And he raced after Greely.

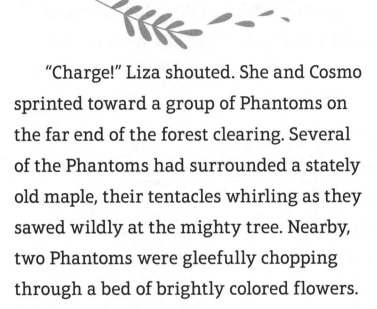

"Charge!" Liza shouted. She and Cosmo sprinted toward a group of Phantoms on the far end of the forest clearing. Several of the Phantoms had surrounded a stately old maple, their tentacles whirling as they sawed wildly at the mighty tree. Nearby, two Phantoms were gleefully chopping through a bed of brightly colored flowers.

The Phantom duo sneered at Liza and Cosmo as they drew near. "Ahhh, you're just in time," one of them said, his voice dripping with sarcasm. "I'm Wart. While our friends destroy the maple tree, we're preparing a little Welcome to Jamaa party for the Phantom King. My friend Reek and I decided to cut ourselves some flowers for decorations."

Liza looked up at her Alpha Stone on the end of her staff. Cosmo's Alpha Stone was on his staff, too, located on the side of his horn. The two Alphas shared a look of understanding between them and seconds later, the Alpha Stones began to glow.

Reek gave the Alphas a wicked smile. "Aren't they sssssweet?" he hissed, holding up a cluster of sagging green stems with the blossoms chopped off. "We're gonna cut all the flowers for the Phantom King. Bye bye, flowersssss."

Cosmo was filled with a rush of anger. He knew how Peck felt when she'd gasped a few minutes earlier. How could anyone treat plants this way? His eyes fell on the woody shrub behind Wart and Reek. It was covered with pink flowers shaped like trumpets. The petals fluttered gently. He understood they were trying to tell him something, and for a moment, Cosmo let his anger slip away. Instead, he focused on the Alpha Stone. He could feel the power growing as he strained to understand the message the flowers were trying to give him.

"Maybe we could use that thing he's holding for a vase," Reek said, jutting his chin. The Phantom was staring at Cosmo's horn-topped staff with an unblinking eye.

"We like candles," Wart cackled, reaching toward Cosmo's candle with a spindly tentacle. "We like how they burn things."

A wind began to blow, stirring the petals on the ground. "Think again," Cosmo said calmly as the wind continued to grow. Suddenly the air was filled with thousands of petals blowing this way and that.

"Ahhh!" Wart cried out as petals blew into his eye and stuck to the oozing gunk. "I can't see!"

Liza's gaze swiveled to the left and then to the right, sizing up the situation. This was her chance to strike. "The only thing getting burned from now on is YOU," Liza yelled, darting behind Reek and Wart to attack the unsuspecting Phantoms at the tree. Using her wooden staff, the brave panda Alpha twisted it this way and that, knocking the Phantoms to the ground. Whack! Whack! Whack! Liza moved so quickly that the Phantoms, caught off guard, couldn't get out of her way fast enough. Her braid bounced on her back as she ran across the petal-covered ground.

Reek and Wart were so busy struggling with the flying petals that they didn't notice Liza had raced off—or that Cosmo had reached into the pocket of his moss skirt and pulled out a handful of spiky green boomseeds—small seeds that exploded when they made contact with something.

"I hate to break it to you fellows, but guess what? Party's over!" Cosmo shouted. Boom! He threw the boomseeds at Reek and Wart, sending them running for cover. Immediately, the wind died down. Petals floated softly back to the ground. "Thank you," Cosmo said to the flowers that were still standing. "You are brave warriors indeed."

Instinctively he could feel the flowers

thanking him back. Words like *grateful* and *thankful* and *defender* entered his mind.

The courage of the Alphas and the fear of more boomseeds had the desired effect. The Phantoms had halted their attack on the maple tree. Their tentacles stopped turning and they quickly slithered backward. With victory in sight, Liza and Cosmo grinned at each other, and together chased after them.

CHAPTER SIX

Pine needles were raining down from the sky when Peck leaped into the middle of the chaos. Graham was already swinging across the clearing on a vine, ready to execute a plan. Where should she focus? Everywhere she turned, Phantoms were causing pandemonium. A few of them had wrapped their gangly tentacles around the tree trunks and were squeezing hard.

"You're trying to kill the trees by giving them bear hugs?" Peck shrieked, incredulous. "No, no, no! That is not happening!" Taking a deep breath, Peck held up the paintbrush holding her Alpha Stone.

Peck gazed intently at her Alpha Stone and called upon the natural forces of Jamaa for help. Within seconds she felt a tingling energy—and a rush of inspiration. She quickly gathered up some of the fallen pine needles. Peck was known for always coming up with ideas, and her Alpha Stone's power helped her harness her creativity. In a flash, she braided needles together, forming a long, thin whip.

Peck brandished the whip at the Phantoms. Then, like lightning, she lashed out. Whoosh! The thin whip snapped at the Phantoms' spindly tentacles. "There's more where that came from so stay back!" Peck cried, cracking it again. The Phantoms spun in circles, not sure where to go.

"There's a lot more of us than there are of you," said one of the Phantoms she had hit, his beady little eye glaring at her. His back tentacle reached out to snatch the whip. But Peck, already anticipating his move, did a quick backflip, moving just out of his reach.

The Phantoms were clearly irritated by the whip. And sure, it stung. But it wasn't enough to scare them off. Suddenly Peck remembered something that Greely had once told her. Phantoms didn't like music—of any kind. So she began to sing as loudly as she could. "Everything in Jamaa is beautiful! The rivers and the lakes, the mountains and the forests . . . it's a paradise, it's a perfect place, and we're not gonna let you take over . . . no no no, no no no!" She began clapping her paws and swaying from side to side.

The Phantoms had stopped their destruction. They were wincing in pain and shaking slightly. A few of them had fled into the forest. Her plan was working!

"Is my singing really that bad?" she sang at the top of her lungs as more Phantoms slithered off. "'Cause if it is, I'm so, so glad!"

Like a gymnast, Graham swung across the treetops of the clearing, using the vines as ropes. From his vantage spot above the others, he had seen Liza ably battling the Phantoms at the base of an old maple tree. He could hear Phantoms yelling out in agony in the direction Cosmo had run. And was that Peck . . . singing? Whatever she was doing, it seemed to be working.

Graham was confident that his fellow Alphas were in control. He focused his attention now on where the biggest clusters of Phantoms were—the sections of the clearing that were in the most danger.

Graham saw a huge cluster of Phantoms traveling as a group. They were pulling up flowers and mowing down shrubs.

"Scary stuff down there. Good thing I'm up here," he whispered. Because he was up in the branches, the agile monkey Alpha was surrounded by hundreds of tree nuts. They were each about the size of a plum. And they were very hard.

He reached in his backpack and pulled out his handmade slingshot. Next, he began pulling nuts off the branches. He loaded one in the slingshot. And then he let it loose.

Blast! One of the Phantoms fell hard onto its side, sending the other Phantoms around him flying. It was a perfect hit. He gave his Alpha Stone a reassuring squeeze, and then with rapid-fire precision, Graham fired off nut after nut. He hit Phantoms on the back. On the head. And in their beady bulbous eyes. The Phantoms were spinning wildly, smashing into one another in their confusion. Several of them fell onto their backs, their tentacles kicking violently in the air.

Two of the Phantoms were shouting, trying to regain order in their ranks. They hopped up onto a boulder, their tentacles waving the other Phantoms over. Graham held his slingshot steady as he listened closely. "This battle must end for now," one of the Phantoms screeched. His eye was bulging with rage.

The other Phantom took over. "But we know who will win in the end," he bellowed, holding his tentacles wide. "No more wasting time here . . . we have work to do."

The Phantoms that remained in the clearing began scurrying out of the glade, after the two Phantom leaders.

Graham swiftly dropped to the ground, shoving his slingshot back in his backpack.

"We did it!" Liza said as the dust settled and the Alphas came together in the clearing.

"Oh my gosh, Graham, that nut slingshot was the best," Peck said delightedly. "When we get back to Alphas Hollow can you show me how to make one?"

But Graham wasn't paying attention. Instead, he ran over to the old maple tree

Liza had defended and scaled the bark to the top. He stood on a branch, shielding his eyes from the sun, searching the land.

"What is it?" Cosmo yelled up. "What do you see?"

A few seconds later, Graham came scrabbling down the trunk. "The Phantoms might have left this clearing, but they all seem to be headed in the same direction," he said, wild-eyed. Little tufts of fur stood up at odd angles on his head, and his goggles were crooked. "Straight toward the rainforest—they're headed toward Mt. Magma."

"The volcano?" Peck asked, her paws on her hips. "Why would the Phantoms be going there?" Mt. Magma sat on the edge of the jungle, near the Lost Temple of Zios.

Liza nodded. "The fact that they didn't

disappear into a portal, and that they're still here in Jamaa makes me incredibly nervous."

"I don't know why they're headed toward the volcano—or why they're back in Jamaa," Graham said worriedly, looking at the others. "But we'd better find out."

Toucans flew overhead as Cosmo, Graham, Liza, and Peck tracked the Phantoms toward Mt. Magma. The trail had taken the four Alphas through the heart of Sarepia Forest. A thick canopy of tree leaves masked the sunlight from shining through.

"Are you sure this is the way?" Peck asked as they walked down a muddy footpath. "I taught an art class over here once, and I can't tell you how many times I got lost. By the time I got there, I had only twenty minutes to teach an entire lesson on watercolors!"

Liza took in the mud-covered trail and frowned in dismay. "Peck's right," she said. For a while the Alphas had been following the trail of rotten goop, decayed plants, and terrible smells the Phantoms had left in their wake. But now, there was nothing—no rot or mold, no deadly fumes, and no signs that anyone had been here recently. "I think maybe we should have turned left back there, where we saw those wild mushrooms growing. If the Phantoms had come this way, they would have left a stinky trail."

A bright yellow butterfly landed on top of Graham's head. "I could climb up to the top of the tree canopy," he suggested, rubbing his beard. "But I'm not sure I'm going to be able to see very much. You know what they say: big leaves, small views!"

Suddenly a large nut appeared out of nowhere, thudding at the Alphas' feet. And a few seconds later, thud! Another one landed. They were the size of apples.

"We're under attack!" Peck cried, spinning around, bracing for a fight.

"Haha, that's no attack, Peck," Cosmo said, his face lighting up. "We're safe. The trees are just trying to get our attention." He pointed behind her. "Look." Sure enough, a cluster of towering nut trees were shaking their limbs in the Alphas' direction.

The Alphas hurried over to the trees. "You speak nut, right, Cosmo?" Graham asked. "I wish I did!"

"You don't have to speak nut when you

are a nut," Cosmo joked, chuckling. Peck let out a giggle, too—it felt good to lighten the mood, if only for a minute.

Cosmo wrapped his arms and body around one of the trees. A dreamy smile came over his face.

"I'm definitely putting this in a picture frame," Liza said good-naturedly, taking a photo. "Caption: Tree Hugger!"

"And proud of it," Cosmo replied, hopping off and dusting himself off. "Okay, here's what I just learned—the trees want us to know that we have to take the path over there, like Liza thought," he said, pointing to the left of where they'd been headed.

"Is that where the Phantoms went?" Peck asked, rubbing her paws together in anticipation. Her violet eyes shone. "I'm ready to kick some more Phantom butt!"

CHAPTER SEVEN

"I would have appreciated knowing we were headed to Crystal Sands," Sir Gilbert said, his tone clipped as he and Greely stood side-by-side on a sandy beach. The air was hot and the sun was shining, as it always did in Crystal Sands. The two Alphas had found a secluded spot along the miles of shoreline. "A little clarity would have been warmly welcomed."

"I didn't want to waste more time," Greely replied, his eyes focused on the clear blue ocean. "These waters are known for their pearls. Dive in and find one. I'll keep watch on the shore."

Sir Gilbert bristled at being ordered around. "Might I say, it was your idea to come here, Greely. Why don't *you* dive in?"

"I'd prefer not to," Greely replied. The unapproachable wolf Alpha looked both out of place and uncomfortable in the relaxed setting.

"Oh, that is rich," Sir Gilbert said incredulously. "You would prefer not to." He gave Greely a withering glance. "And may I add, finding a pearl might not be a simple task. It is not as if the pearls will be easily visible. As they would have been at Epic Wonders," he sniped, unable to resist.

"We're wasting time," Greely snapped.

Sir Gilbert's ears pulled back. "It is very clear to me now. One of us needs to take action. Evidently, it will be me."

Holding his head high, Sir Gilbert glided into the water. He gave a regal nod back at Greely, and he swore he saw a hint of a smile break the wolf Alpha's usually inscrutable face. When the water was deep enough, he dove in.

The water felt refreshingly cool, and Sir Gilbert was glad he, not Greely, was searching for the pearl. His powerful legs propelled him deeper and deeper into the water, and when he reached the white sandy bottom below, his eyes scanned the ocean floor. Using his sharp claws, he grabbed a cluster of mollusks and swam back to the shore.

"I suppose you expect me to open them, too," he said, taking a breath after dropping the mollusks on the sand near

Greely. The wolf hadn't moved. Sir Gilbert shook the water from his fur, purposely trying to get Greely wet.

Greely then did something unexpected. "I will help," he said, and together they began to open the shells. One by one they pried the mollusks open and found nothing but pebbles and sand. Finally, one unopened mollusk lay on the ground between them.

Greely laid his paw on the hard shell. "Shall I do the honors?" he asked drily.

"Please do," Sir Gilbert replied. "But I have to say, the chances of this last mollusk containing a pearl—"

The tiger Alpha was interrupted with a sharp crack as Greely snapped open the shell.

There, glinting and shimmering, was a

smooth white pearl.

"What were you saying?" Greely asked. And there was no mistaking it this time— spreading across the wolf Alpha's face was a full grin.

The trail was downhill—and steep. The farther the four Alphas went, the darker it grew. Before long, the light had all but disappeared and darkness surrounded them.

As the Alphas walked, they kept looking behind them—and peering into the darkness. There was no sign of the Phantoms, but that only made them more suspicious.

"They've got to be here somewhere. We're almost at Mt. Magma!" Peck whispered, stepping on a branch. *Crack!*

The sound shattered the silence.

The Alphas stopped walking and stood silently in the rainforest. It felt as if hundreds of eyes were watching them. Were they?

Cosmo wiped some rain droplets from his fur. "We definitely are on the right track. But you know how devious and sneaky Phantoms are. They could be under our feet, for all we know." With that, everyone looked down at the ground. They'd been scanning the path for hidden traps—nets and webs—but so far, nothing.

"What's this?" Liza asked, brushing aside some long, stringy vines. Underneath was something very strange: a moss-covered stone wall. She pushed aside some vines to reveal more of the wall.

"What's a wall doing in the middle of

the rainforest?" Peck wondered aloud.

Graham stared intently at the stone. Then he scampered down next to it and began running his hands over the structure. "The Phantoms want us to think this is a wall," he said slowly. "But the minute they want us to think one way, I think the opposite!" The monkey held up a fistful of vines. "Bingo! It's a door." Underneath the vines, barely visible in the stone, were the slight outlines of hinges.

"Okay, you're definitely a genius," Peck said, offering Graham a fist bump. Graham blinked in confusion, and then put his hand over her paw, making Peck giggle. She pulled her paw back and then lightly tapped his fist with hers. "And geniuses need to learn how to fist bump!"

"Stories where characters find secret

passageways and hidden doors are my favorite," Cosmo said, reaching up in awe to touch the hinges. "I never thought I'd actually help discover one myself!"

"How do we get inside?" Liza asked, scanning the wall door for a way in.

"And what are we going to find if we do?" Peck wondered.

Graham didn't answer. Instead he was busily pulling on the vines that covered the wall, gently testing each one. He mumbled under his breath. "Not this one. Okay. How about this one? No." Then he pulled on a curled, climbing strand.

The hidden door slowly swung open.

"You did it!" Peck said.

This time, Graham offered her a fist bump, then flashed her an appreciative smile. "Any inventor worth his salt knows that if there's a door, there's a way in. Just might take some time to find it."

The Alphas peered inside. A twisting passageway led into the darkness.

Liza stepped forward. "Let's do this."

Cosmo lit the candle at the end of his staff, then joined Liza. "The flame can help show us the way," he said, holding it up. The light flickered in front of them.

Peck scooted closer to Liza. "Secret passages in the dark aren't my favorite," she whispered to Liza as the Alphas stepped into the secret passageway. The door swung slowly shut behind them.

The passageway was narrow and sloped downward. There wasn't room for the Alphas to walk side-by-side. They had to walk single file, casting eerie shadows on the stone walls that loomed up on either side of them. If not for the flickering glow of Cosmo's candle, they would have been in utter darkness.

"Do you hear that?" Liza said softly, halting her step. Everyone stood silent, listening. There was a clanking, and a faint whirring noise that seemed to be coming from below.

"Clanking and whirring and clashing . . . it sounds like some kind of machine," Graham whispered. "And machines don't belong in the middle of the rainforest." The Alphas exchanged worried glances.

The Alphas began moving forward once more. They began to hear the faint sounds of voices, which were frantic and agitated.

"Phantoms," Liza whispered, motioning them to keep going. The passageway turned. When they came around the corner, the wall on their left was lowered enough so that the Alphas could make out light coming from below.

Cosmo blew out his candle so they wouldn't be seen. The four Alphas crept to the wall, making sure to stay out of the sight line of anyone who might be below them.

They raised their heads and peered over the edge of the wall, not quite knowing what to expect. Much to their surprise, they were standing on the edge of an enormous cavern.

"Watch your step, folks! We're on the edge of the crater," Graham whispered as everyone realized the same thing at once: The secret path had actually taken them *inside* Mt. Magma! He gazed around in wonder. "I've always wondered what it looked like inside a volcano." Far above them, a small sliver of sky was visible from the tip of the volcano. Below them was the volcano's floor. And there, in the middle of the volcano, was an army of Phantoms hard at work.

Some of the Phantoms were digging into Mt. Magma's base, using their tentacles to shovel dirt away from the chamber walls. Others were chipping away at the ground, removing layer after layer of dirt.

Large maps lay spread out on tables on the far side of the cavern. Clusters of Phantoms were studying the maps and talking among themselves, wildly gesturing with their tentacles.

"Lava," Peck said softly, her eyes wide. Sure enough, in the very middle of the dig site there was a small burble of lava visible. It was boiling hot, bubbling and fuming. A few Phantoms stood by it, fanning it with gigantic leaves. The more they fanned, the more fumes and bubbles there were.

A very large Phantom was making the rounds, inspecting the work of the smaller Phantoms. His black body was covered with purple splotches, and the top of his head was cracked open. It almost looked like he was wearing a crown. And unlike the worker Phantoms, who all seemed to have multiple pairs of tentacles, this Phantom only had two.

Cosmo gasped. "It's the Phantom King!"

"Shhh, listen," Liza murmured as she took pictures. They couldn't risk missing a single word.

"This is going exactly as I dreamed," the Phantom King said to one of his henchmen, a fat, bulbous Phantom with hairy tentacles. The Phantom King's loud, gleeful voice echoed off the chamber's walls. "The summer solstice is tomorrow. Now that we've exposed the lava, the sun and sky will unite and the volcano will erupt." He let out a booming laugh, and his henchman laughed back. "Soon all of this wretched land will be covered with hot lava. Trees will burn. Lakes will be filled with ash. And the fields will wear a coat of crunchy molten rock. It's going to be so beautiful."

"And the animals?" the henchman asked, a revolting grin taking over his entire face. "Tell me about the animals."

The Phantom King chuckled, flexing his muscled tentacles. With each move, ripples of electricity shot up and down them. "Every village they have built will be destroyed. Their civilization will be in ruins. And any animal who isn't burned by the lava will suffocate in the rain of ash that will befall this land. Soon the animals will be nothing more than a footnote in the history of Jamaa. A mere fable, a sad story." His eye pulsed with giddy anticipation. "Mt. Magma will be the end of every animal species. Which means one thing. Finally, Jamaa will be back with its rightful ruler. ME!"

CHAPTER EIGHT

"One riddle down, two to go," Sir Gilbert said, feeling determined. He had strung the pearl from a bit of string they found by the beach, and it now bounced against his chest as they walked.

The forest path they were on was covered with twigs and leaves, yet Greely managed to walk without making a single sound. In fact, Sir Gilbert turned around every ten yards or so just to make sure that Greely was still with him. This seemed to bother the wolf.

"Do you think I'm going to disappear?" Greely asked quietly after the seventh time Sir Gilbert had turned to check.

"One never knows," Sir Gilbert said haughtily, staring at him for a long moment. Throwing his shoulders back, he faced forward again and continued along the path. "'I hang from the sky and lie on the ground. I am closed or open, long or small,'" Sir Gilbert said to himself, hoping that it would help him think of the answer.

"Instead of repeating the riddle over and over, we need to solve it," Greely muttered from behind him.

"I am well aware of that fact, thank you," Sir Gilbert said crisply over his shoulder. Greely was certainly not easy to get along with.

Dusk would be falling soon. "Let me remind you, if it were not for me, we would not have solved the first riddle."

For the first time that day, Greely stepped on a branch. Snap. Sir Gilbert knew that he'd gotten under the wolf Alpha's skin. And then, in a burst of frustration, Greely kicked at a pinecone, sending it flying through the woods.

"No need to throw things," Sir Gilbert scolded as another pinecone came sailing past his face.

Whoosh! Without warning, Greely leaped past Sir Gilbert and landed next to the pinecone. He picked it up and held it in front of the tiger Alpha.

"It's a pinecone."

Sir Gilbert blinked. "Very good, Greely. But now is not the time for a nature lesson—"

Greely cut him off. "Pinecones are on the branches above us and on the ground under us. Some of them are closed, some of them are open."

"And they can be long or small," Sir Gilbert finished, realizing where Greely was going with this. "You did it! You solved the second riddle!"

Greely fashioned a string from long blades of grass. He wrapped one end of the string around the pinecone and tied the other end to the chain he wore around his neck.

"One riddle left," Sir Gilbert said elatedly. "One answer stands between us getting Mira back!"

"This is far worse than I'd imagined,"

Cosmo said as he and the other Alphas raced back up the narrow passageway. Now that they had heard the Phantoms' plans, they were impatient to get back outside, where they could figure out their next steps.

"I feel sick to my stomach," Peck confessed as they rounded the corner. Her earring jingled as she ran. "All this Phantom activity must have polluted the ground water leading to Bunny Burrow!"

"And Bunny Burrow won't be the only place affected by the Phantom King's plan. All of Jamaa is in danger!" Graham added as the Alphas reached the hidden door. The Alphas pushed on the door and it swung open. They spilled out into the fading daylight.

Liza paced back and forth. "We need to come up with a plan that's going to stop the

Phantoms, once and for all."

"It's time to get the strength of all of the Alphas together. We need to find Greely and Sir Gilbert," Cosmo said, snapping his fingers. "That's our best chance for a positive outcome."

"You're right," Liza said, nodding. A look of determination came over her face. "And time is running out."

"Let's go back to Alphas Hollow," Peck suggested. "Surely we can think of something!"

Dusk had begun to fall as the panda, monkey, bunny, and koala Alphas ran through the woods toward Alphas Hollow.

Peck glanced up at the darkening sky and noticed something flying in the air above them. Whatever it was, it looked too big to be a bat. Peck squinted, slowing down her pace. "Guys, stop for a minute," she called to the other Alphas, who were behind her. Then she cupped her paws around her mouth. "Ivan! It's Peck—and I'm with Cosmo, Liza, and Graham. Can you fly down to us for a minute? We need your help!"

Ivan swooped toward the ground and landed on a tree branch near the Alphas.

"Peck, hello," Ivan said. "Good to see you again." The stately eagle greeted the other Alphas. "I was just enjoying the breeze on this last night before the solstice. How can I help you?"

"We found out that the Phantom army has infiltrated Mt. Magma," Peck explained, waving her paws. "They've been digging out layers of dirt to expose the lava, and at the moment of solstice tomorrow, their plan is to cause the volcano to erupt."

"They're messing with nature," Cosmo said, his shoulders sagging. "It's so wrong."

A shudder went through the Alphas.

"What can I do?" Ivan asked, alarmed at seeing the Alphas so upset.

"We need to find Greely and Sir Gilbert," Peck told him. "Have you seen them?"

Ivan nodded. "I was with them earlier today. I'm sure I can find them."

"We have to find them," Peck exclaimed. She threw her arms open wide as her words grew more impassioned. "All the Alphas need to be together!"

"I'll do some quick calculations and fly to where I think Greely and Sir Gilbert should be," Ivan said. "When I find them, I will tell them what you've told me. Where should they meet you?"

The Alphas looked at one another. For now, they had planned to go back to Alphas Hollow—but that wouldn't be the best place for Greely and Sir Gilbert to meet them. It would waste time that they didn't have. "Tell them that they should meet us in the morning at the volcano," Liza said as the others nodded. "We'll be waiting for them there at dawn."

Ivan bowed his head. "I will do whatever I can to help you." The eagle flapped his powerful wings and disappeared into the night sky.

Greely was never in the best of moods, and now was no exception. He and Sir Gilbert had spent hours exploring and searching the lands of Jamaa, but had turned up nothing. It didn't help that neither of the Alphas had any idea what they were looking for. This had begun to gnaw at him.

Greely didn't like not knowing things.

"Perhaps we should visit Mt. Shiveer," Sir Gilbert suggested. "We haven't explored any terrain there. If we run, we can get there quickly."

"Perhaps we shouldn't," Greely muttered sourly. What good would going to Mt. Shiveer do? The pompous tiger Alpha had made one impractical suggestion after the next, and in Greely's mind, all of them were worthless. The clock was ticking. There wasn't time to go to Mt. Shiveer. There wasn't time for anything.

Crack! A bolt of lightning flashed in the

sky above the forest. Sir Gilbert paused. "All right, Greely. Since you have rejected my many futile attempts to solve the third riddle, enlighten me, my friend. Surely, it seems, you must have the answer. What do you think we should do?"

Greely glared at him. "If I had the answer, we wouldn't be standing out here in the forest, would we?"

Sir Gilbert bristled, his mouth twisting into a frown. "Then I suggest that for once you attempt to be, if not agreeable, then at least civil. I am quite certain I don't have to remind you that working together is the best road to success."

"And you call this success?" Greely grumbled, looking darkly at the forest as a heavy rain began to pour down. The wolf Alpha angrily strode from tree to tree. "Going to Mt. Shiveer would get us nowhere," Greely told him. "You have no idea what we're even looking for."

Sir Gilbert's voice rose in anger. "We are looking for an answer that will save all of Jamaa, Greely. Even someone as hard-hearted as you knows that Jamaa's future is resting on our shoulders."

Greely sighed in frustration. "I'd be better off on my own."

Raindrops landed on the thick canopy of leaves above them. Thunder boomed in the sky. Any fleeting happiness Greely had felt after solving the second riddle had been replaced with something else.

Despair.

"You might be . . . but would Jamaa?" Sir Gilbert shouted. "For once, Greely, stop thinking about yourself."

Anger coursed through Greely's veins. If that was what Sir Gilbert thought, Greely wasn't about to correct him—even though the tiger Alpha couldn't have been more wrong. "One of us has to think," he growled instead, stalking toward him. His sopping dark purple cloak clung to his body.

The two Alphas faced off. Exhausted, cold, and hungry, they glared at each other, each holding his ground in the driving rain. Lightning crashed and thunder boomed. Rivers of water ran down the animals' fur, dripping from their whiskers. The ground under their feet was soon a muddy mess. Stubbornness and pride took up the space between them.

And then, suddenly, as they glowered at each other, soaked to the skin, they each had an identical, startling, simultaneous realization.

In unison, the two Alphas whispered, "Sometimes I'm fast, and sometimes I'm slow. I always fall but won't stand up, I'm free for all but can't be bought."

Greely's irises flickered. And Sir Gilbert gasped.

The answer to Mira's riddle was all around them. Rain. The answer to the third riddle was rain.

CHAPTER NINE

Back at the Alphas Hollow, the four Alphas hashed out the details of how they'd take the Phantom Army and the Phantom King down.

Liza sat at the Alphas' large round wooden table, scrolling through the photographs she had taken when the Alphas had been inside Mt. Magma. "As far as I can tell, there's only one way in—and one way out," she said. "That makes our mission a little easier."

"That's a good thought, but we don't know for sure. There could be other secret entrances," Graham said. He had emptied the contents of his backpack on the floor and was tossing things he didn't need.

"Do you think there are other secret doors?" Peck wondered. She was lying on her side, propped up on one elbow.

"There's no way of knowing," Liza said. "We'll just have to prepare for anything."

"I had an idea when we were walking back to the Hollow," Cosmo said, taking a sip of hot cocoa. "I was remembering the long-ago epic battle when Jamaa was saved from the Phantoms. How at first things weren't going our way, but when we all worked together, everything clicked."

Graham nodded. "That's how we won."

Peck jumped to her feet. "That's how we'll defeat the Phantoms! We need to get all of the animals to fight alongside us now, too! If we can get everyone fired up, there won't be any stopping us!" She jumped to her feet. "I'll run over to Bunny Burrow now and tell the bunnies. They can spread the word for us!"

"I agree," Cosmo said, feeding off Peck's energy. "If we split up and ask the animals to help us, we should be able to get all the species to meet at the volcano door by morning." He paused. "But it can't just be the four of us. We need Sir Gilbert and Greely."

"They'll be there," Peck said confidently. "Ivan won't let us down. And neither will they."

It was still dark in the predawn hour when Sir Gilbert and Greely arrived back at Coral Canyons. They had walked all night to their destination, and Coral Canyons was completely quiet. The two of them had prowled around the area, finally settling next to the pool of water. The blue-gray marble statue of Mira looked like nothing more than a statue.

Sir Gilbert was lying down, staring at the horizon. Slowly, the sky around him began to lighten. A small red bead of light shone in the distance—the sun. Neither of them had said a word since they had returned to Coral Canyons. But unlike before, the silence hadn't been uncomfortable. After solving the final riddle together, there was new calmness between them.

"Soon it will be daybreak," Greely said, breaking the silence. His gaze flickered down to the statue of Mira and to the still water of the pool. No spray shot from the spout. No ripples fluttered across the surface.

Yet.

Sir Gilbert looked at the space between them. There, on a low, flat rock, sat the pearl and the pinecone. And next to them was a small pail they had found hanging from a tree, meant to collect sap. They had filled it with rainwater and carried it here.

Sir Gilbert sighed. "I don't know how you do it," he said to Greely.

Greely arched one of the white tufts of fur above his eye. "Do what?" he asked.

The tiger stretched. "Keep so many secrets. You are quite the enigma, you know," he said. "Spending most of your time alone, far away from everyone." He chuckled. "The other animals don't know what to make of you. I daresay they are a little frightened of you. But I know you are not as mysterious as you set out to be. Thank you for your help. I—I am not sure I could have accomplished Mira's task without you."

Greely merely stared back at Sir Gilbert with a puzzled look on his face. "Interesting," he said flatly.

Sir Gilbert sighed. "Moving on, then, I suppose." He glanced down at the ring containing his red Alpha Stone. "It is getting warmer. The sun is rising."

Greely moved and the dark blue Alpha Stone on the leather cuff on his front leg glinted in the sunlight.

"Our Alpha Stones will be strongest at the exact moment of solstice," Sir Gilbert declared. He was used to having conversations like this with Greely. For every three or four things Sir Gilbert said, he would get a single nod or shrug.

But Greely surprised him now. "We will not have to wait much longer," Greely said, watching the sun climb into the sky. Despite his fellow Alpha's gruff demeanor, Sir Gilbert could tell Greely was looking forward to Mira's potential return to Jamaa.

Something overhead caught Sir Gilbert's eye. It was Ivan the eagle, flying very fast. Instantly Sir Gilbert knew that the eagle was on an important mission.

Sir Gilbert leaped up to stand by Greely as the eagle swooped down frantically in front of them.

"What is it?" Greely asked, staring intently at Ivan.

The eagle took large, painful gulps of

air, trying to steady himself. "The other Alphas. Cosmo, Liza, Peck, and Graham. They—they sent me to get you."

"Why?" Sir Gilbert demanded. "Are they hurt?"

Ivan shook his head, his feathers quivering. "No. It's the Phantoms. They've invaded Mt. Magma. They're trying to get the volcano to erupt at the exact moment of the solstice," Ivan sputtered, taking a breath. "The Phantoms want to destroy everything and make the Phantom King ruler of what's left of Jamaa!"

Greely let out a ferocious howl. The horrible sound echoed across the canyon.

"Where are the other Alphas?" Sir Gilbert asked, his whiskers taut.

"They will be at Mt. Magma," Ivan said, looking from Greely to Sir Gilbert. "They were going to be waiting for you there at dawn."

"What?" Sir Gilbert cried. "The only chance we have to help Mira come back to Jamaa is now!" the regal tiger Alpha shouted. "Today, when the sun will be at its highest point."

Greely was striding back and forth, back and forth, snarling. "I can't let Mira down."

"*We. We* can't let her down," Sir Gilbert roared angrily. "We've done everything she asked. This might be our only chance to ever get her back! We cannot leave!"

"So what should we do, then?" Greely hissed, coming face-to-face with Sir Gilbert. "Let the Phantom King take over Jamaa? Is that what you're saying?"

"No! Of course not!" Sir Gilbert smacked his paw furiously into the dirt.

"This is an unbearable choice."

Suddenly mist rose from the pool. The marble statue glowed with a soft light, and water began to spray from the fountainhead.

"Mira," Greely whispered, sprinting to the edge of the water.

"You have come back to us," Sir Gilbert cried, joining him. "But we are in a terrible predicament. We've just learned that the Phantoms have invaded Mt. Magma and that the other Alphas need our help. Ivan—"

"Yes, Sir Gilbert. I know," Mira's mystical voice interrupted the tiger Alpha's worries.

"We cannot leave without you—but we cannot let the Phantoms take over," Sir Gilbert declared as Greely stood silently next to him, hoping for some guidance from their guardian spirit.

The water glistened as Mira's celestial

voice spoke to them. "Sir Gilbert. Greely. There is only one true choice. You must join the other Alphas. You must save Jamaa."

Greely lowered his gaze, realizing what that would mean.

"But—but the riddles have all been answered," Sir Gilbert protested. "We have the pearl, the pinecone, and the rainwater. All the things we need to help you return to us, Mira. As you said—the alignment of the planets means that this year's solstice is a once-in-a-lifetime opportunity." Now that his hopes had been raised, he couldn't bear to let the dream of having Mira back in Jamaa perish.

The water shone bright now, the sun's rays bouncing off the surface. "You did everything you were asked to do, and I am proud of you," Mira said, gently. "Yet, how can I come back if Jamaa is in ruins?" Mira's voice was tinged with sadness.

"We will do whatever you wish," Greely said, raising his gaze to look directly at the statue. "Always."

"And I hope one day we have another chance to be together. But, you must always remember what I am about to tell you." Now Mira sounded resolute. "The world of Jamaa is more important than I," she said. "And it is more important than you." The water rippled. "Your fellow animals, and your fellow *Alphas*, are more important than anything. Never forget that." She paused for a moment. "And never forget this: I will always be with you."

The mist vanished. The water smoothed. And the glow around the statue of Mira disappeared.

Greely turned to Sir Gilbert. "We must go." He looked up at Ivan, whose beak hung open, stunned at what he had just seen. "Fly back to Sarepia Forest. Tell the other eagles—all the animals—that we will need everyone's help. We will not be defeated."

Greely glanced back at the now quiet fountain. "Not after this sacrifice," he murmured.

Sir Gilbert closed his eyes. Then he nodded toward the pail. "Drink before you go. We—we do not need the rainwater anymore."

Ivan obliged by taking several sips. Then, he flapped his wings and soared up into the bright blue sky. Greely and Sir Gilbert locked eyes, grabbed the pearl and pinecone respectively, and without saying a word, dashed toward Mt. Magma.

CHAPTER TEN

"They should be here by now!" Peck whispered impatiently. She and the other three Alphas were outside Mt. Magma, waiting for Sir Gilbert and Greely to arrive. But the four Alphas weren't alone. Hundreds of animals had heard the Alphas' battle cry—and had rallied to the volcano to help save Jamaa. Raccoons clutched rocks to defend themselves. Lemurs leaped around in anticipation, ready to claw the Phantoms with their nails. Deer clustered together, prepared to run forward and charge as a group. Every species in Jamaa was ready for battle.

Liza bit her lip. "Come on, come on," she said to herself, looking up at the sky. The solstice would soon be here. Where were the missing Alphas?

Cosmo tilted his head upward, listening for a sign from the jungle.

"What is it, Cosmo? Do you hear something?" Peck asked, her long ears perking up.

"The trees promised they'd let me know when Greely and Sir Gilbert are near us," Cosmo explained, wringing his paws. "There's no sign of them."

Graham was huddled with a group of monkeys, teaching them how to make slingshots using branches and nuts. Soon there was a crowd of enthusiastic monkeys newly armed with slingshots. They hopped about, eager to let their ammunition fly.

The Alphas heard a commotion coming from the jungle. Branches began to shake and twigs snapped loudly.

"Is it Greely and Sir Gilbert?" Peck asked Cosmo as a group of bunnies huddled around her.

Cosmo shook his head, looking pained. "Phantoms," he whispered.

The Phantom army's tentacles hacked at branches and vines as they marched through the forest. But when they saw the animals and Alphas, they stopped, momentarily stunned. Phantoms faced off against the animals and the Alphas.

Liza stepped forward, unafraid. "We know what you're up to inside the volcano," she boldly told them.

"Yeah, we're on to you. And it's not going to work!" Peck added, puffing out her chest. "If you know what's good for you, you'll give up now!" The bunnies around her all nodded.

The Phantoms looked at one another and began to chuckle. "What's this?" one of them said sarcastically, holding up his tentacles in mock horror. "A bunny and a koala? Oooh, I'm so scared."

"When will you silly little animals realize that you can't stop us?" one of the Phantoms shouted out, pushing a raccoon aside. "No one can!"

"Monkeys! Now!" Graham shouted. The monkeys began shooting off their slingshots, raining nuts down on the surprised Phantoms. The deer surged forward, pushing the Phantoms in the direction of the Lost Temple of Zios. At Liza's urging, pandas pelted the enemy with rocks and the bunnies brandished sharpened carrots. Kangaroos hopped on Phantoms, slamming them into the ground. Owls dive-bombed Phantoms while the lemurs began chasing Phantoms in all directions, waving their arms in the air.

"We should head inside the volcano," Liza shouted above the din as a fox chased two Phantoms into the jungle. "The animals have this under control." The others nodded and Graham unlocked the hidden door. They raced inside the passageway toward Mt. Magma.

When the four Alphas rounded the corner and reached the lookout point, what they saw made their hearts sink. Fiery lava was already rising, the molten red liquid bubbling and churning. Phantoms surrounded the lava pit, using fans to blow air onto its boiling surface.

"They're working together," Cosmo exclaimed as the pit belched out puffs of steam.

"Hey, up there!" Graham pointed to the small sliver of sky at the tip of the volcano. Sunlight was coming through.

Peck panicked. "We're too late!" she cried out as the air inside the crater grew hotter. "The solstice is going to happen! Mt. Magma is going to erupt!"

"Calm down, Peck! We can't give up yet!" Liza shouted. "Everyone is counting on us!" Her cry seemed to snap all the Alphas into action. And with that, the battle inside the volcano began.

"Liza's right!" Cosmo said, leaping over

the wall. He raced toward the Phantoms with such force that they stumbled backward, fleeing their posts.

A gust of steam blew Peck's ears backward. "We can do this, guys!" she shouted.

Graham scaled up the crater walls, using the bumps and crevices as footholds. Small vents along the wall were gushing out vapors. "I'm going to climb out the top!" he yelled. "We need to warn the animals that this thing's about to blow!"

Liza realized that the sun was almost at its apex. She leaped over the wall to where several Phantoms were fanning the flames, catching them off guard. Taking her staff, she began striking them, sending them flying into the crater walls.

But she knew that unless all the Alphas

were here, they wouldn't be able to stop the Phantoms, let alone stop the eruption . . .

Without warning, Liza's Alpha Stone began to glow. Liza felt a stirring of power inside her—the strength of all the Alphas combined. The panda Alpha gasped. It could only mean one thing . . .

"RRRRROOOOOAAAAARRRRR!" Sir Gilbert cried, springing over the wall in a smooth, single bound onto a group of Phantoms. He slammed hard into the ground, sending them running for cover. His Alpha Stone glowed a deep, vibrant crimson.

Behind him, Greely bared his sharp teeth. With a growl, he dove through the air, his dark purple cloak blowing backward. The bands on his forelegs smacked against the tentacles of the Phantoms, knocking them perilously close to the bubbling pit. The Phantoms shrieked out in fear, dropping their tools and fleeing, their spindly tentacles waving in the air.

The six Alphas were together at last!

With a collective cheer, the heroes fought side-by-side, driving the Phantoms away from the lava pit and out of the crater. By now, animals had rushed bravely into the crater and were fighting the Phantoms with all their might. Owls beat their wings, confusing the Phantoms. Wolves raced back and forth, causing the Phantoms to scuttle into the recesses of the volcano. Goats used their horns to flip the Phantoms onto their backs. Soon, the courage of all the animal species prevailed. The Phantoms fled the volcano.

"We did it!" Peck cheered as the Alphas gathered around the pit.

But Graham frantically shook his head. "We got rid of the Phantoms—but the volcano is still going to erupt!"

"We've got to get the animals out of here!" Liza cried as steam and smoke filled the air. She and the other Alphas hollered at the animals to run.

"Go! Go!" Sir Gilbert shouted as bunnies, foxes, lynxes, kangaroos, and wolves raced out of the crater.

The six Alphas turned their attention back to the lava. Each of them could feel the energy of their fellow Alphas flowing through their Alpha Stones. They pressed their backs against the inside wall of the crater.

"It's getting so hot," Cosmo said as Peck fanned the air.

Graham's eyes were wide behind his

fogged-up goggles. "Did you feel that? If only I had a seismometer."

"I have a very bad feeling about this," Sir Gilbert pronounced, as Liza nodded grimly. Greely said nothing, but it was clear by his rigid posture that he felt the same way.

A slow, deep hiss echoed throughout the inside of the crater. And then, the boiling red lava began to gurgle and spit.

"It's going to erupt!" Peck cried, her eyes riveted to the scene in front of her. The ground under the Alphas' feet began to tremble, and pieces of rock and shale began to tumble off the crater's walls.

"Here it goes," Cosmo whispered, instinctively bracing for impact. And then, to the Alphas' collective dismay and horror, Mt. Magma erupted in front of them.

Whooosh! Boiling red lava shot upward like an angry geyser, all the way to the top of the crater. Fiery drops of lava sprayed in all directions, hitting the ground just inches in front of where the Alphas stood on the side. The sound of the spurting lava was deafening.

From the sidelines below, Peck gasped. Greely howled.

The Alphas gazed upward feeling helpless, as the molten red geyser reached the top of the volcano.

"The animals outside!" Liza cried out, clutching her camera as Graham shrieked. "Anyone standing near the volcano is going to be hurt!"

Peck was desperately trying to come up with a way to help, but all she could do was take shuddering gulps of hot air.

"We have failed Jamaa," Sir Gilbert said, his voice cracking. The Alphas held their collective breath as the lava seemed to crest the top of the volcano. But then, to their astonishment, it reversed course.

With the same force that had propelled it upward, the lava now streamed back down to the volcano's floor. "Look," Liza breathed. Instead of pooling back into the fiery hot lava pit, it hardened into some sort of figure.

"What's it doing?" Cosmo asked, wide-eyed. Indeed, the lava was forming into a towering statue.

"Is that—is that a bird?" Graham asked, pushing his goggles on top of his head, then back down over his eyes.

"It is not just any bird," Sir Gilbert said quietly, glancing over at Greely, whose expression revealed nothing. "It is our Mira."

The lava had hardened, glowing a bright red, into the extraordinary shape of a twenty-foot tall heron spreading her wings. The bubbling lava that remained at its base gurgled and spewed as it settled down.

"Mira," the six Alphas whispered in unison.

"This is the coolest thing I've ever seen," Peck said, blinking in astonishment.

Soundlessly, Greely moved toward the statue. He gazed up as its features solidified and sharpened. This statue of Mira was much bigger than the one in the pool. But there was no doubt—it was undeniably a manifestation of the guardian spirit.

"The Phantoms thought Jamaa would be covered with lava and that the natural world would be destroyed," Cosmo said, shaking his head in wonderment. "Instead, the eruption of Mt. Magma has given us something amazing!"

"Do you realize—? I mean—? But scientifically—?" Graham sputtered. Finally he was able to string together the words. "The lava is too hot to form into solid rock so quickly—"

"But that's exactly what happened," Liza said, finishing the monkey's thought.

"There was a fountain of Mira in a pool in Coral Canyons," Sir Gilbert announced. "Greely and I both saw it. Two statues of Mira cannot be a coincidence. Truly it is a sign that Mira is always with us."

"There was a statue?" Cosmo asked, his eyes widening.

"And a pool?" Graham threw out his arms. "Tell us everything!"

"Yes, do!" Peck urged, her cheeks pink

from both the heat and from excitement.

"It is quite a story indeed," Sir Gilbert said, his gaze passing from Alpha to Alpha and finally coming to rest on Greely. Greely met his look with the slightest, almost imperceptible, of nods, and an unspoken understanding passed between them. Sir Gilbert knew the wolf didn't want to share the details of what they had experienced with the others just yet, and for once, he felt the same way. "One that deserves the proper time and presentation," Sir Gilbert finished, his tone regal and commanding. "For now, I hope we can agree that this statue will honor Mira's courage and be a place where all in Jamaa can visit and pay her tribute."

Everyone except Greely nodded decisively. The wolf had moved back into the shadows, away from the group.

"Greely? Do you agree with this?" Liza asked.

The wolf's eyes glimmered in the dark. He stepped into the light. "Let's go tell the animals that we are safe."

When the Alphas went back outside, the sun shone bright in the sky and all the animals were celebrating.

"We saw the Phantom King," a group of bunnies exclaimed, hurrying over to greet them. "He disappeared into a portal behind the rest of the Phantoms after the elephants started stomping on him!"

"And the slingshots were rad," an excited trio of monkeys told Graham. "We got rid of a lot of Phantoms with them."

The Alphas smiled at one another. "I

only wish I'd been here to stomp on the Phantom King myself!" Peck said, high-fiving the bunnies. "You guys rock!"

Liza turned to Cosmo and Sir Gilbert. "Who knew that not only would we be celebrating the summer solstice, but that we'd be celebrating saving Jamaa from a volcano?"

"Everyone, please. Listen," Sir Gilbert called out to the animals. "By working together, we have defeated the Phantoms. And in an unexpected twist of fate, the volcano they had hoped would destroy our villages and bring an end to all species of animals has instead turned into our greatest hope."

"The lava formed a statue of Mira inside the crater!" Peck squealed. Animals looked at one another in astonishment, before bursting into wild applause.

"For now, I hope we can agree that this statue will honor Mira's courage and be a place where all in Jamaa can visit and pay her tribute," Sir Gilbert finished. "And we will call it—"

"Mt. Mira," proclaimed Greely, the sound of his voice startling them all. The animals nodded solemnly.

Cosmo broke into a huge smile. "Never a dull moment around here," he told Graham as the animals around them high-fived one another.

Graham nodded. "That was better than any science experiment. I wouldn't have believed it if I hadn't seen it with my own eyes."

"I've got the best idea, guys. I'm going to make Welcome to Mt. Mira T-shirts to hand out at the solstice," Peck said excitedly.

Laughing, Liza nodded. "I love how your mind works, Peck."

Sir Gilbert glanced around. Everyone was smiling and hugging one another . . . except for one Alpha. Sir Gilbert walked over to where Greely stood apart from the others. Something was troubling him. "I'm wondering if we should tell the others about what happened at the fountain," Sir Gilbert said quietly. "We might want to take them there sometime, to see if there might be any further messages from Mira."

To his surprise, Greely shook his shaggy head. "The minute we made our choice to leave the fountain and come to the volcano, we lost the power to communicate with Mira there," he said quietly. "The pool and the fountain are gone."

"You don't know that for sure, Greely," Sir Gilbert chastised. Greely always acted like he knew things the others didn't. It was infuriating.

The wolf Alpha lifted his shoulders in a shrug. "Say and think what you will, Sir Gilbert. We have Mt. Mira. That will have to be enough. For now." And with that, Greely sloped off into the jungle.

The tiger Alpha took a deep breath. He knew the Alphas had a lot to be thankful for. Mira and Zios were watching over them. The volcano eruption had been halted, and Jamaa had been saved. He just wished that Greely could acknowledge what they had gone through.

A bright flash in the air suddenly got his attention and something small landed in front of him. The tiger Alpha peered down to see what it was.

There, sparkling in the grass, was the pearl he and Greely had found together.

Sir Gilbert glanced up and stared through the dark trees. He didn't need to see the wolf Alpha's rippling cloak to know that he was there.

"Everything okay, Sir Gilbert?" Peck asked, bouncing over. She had a hibiscus tucked behind her ear. "You look so serious."

Sir Gilbert chuckled and picked up the shimmering pearl. "Everything's more than fine, Peck. Let's make this summer solstice one for the record books."

Peck clapped her paws. "Sounds like someone wants to join the celebration," she said playfully, putting her small paw in his large one. "And if anyone knows how to bring the party to the party, it's me!"

CONTINUE YOUR

ANIMAL JAM

ADVENTURE!

The story continues online! Uncover this book's code to unlock more fun on www.animaljam.com! Find the letters and numbers engraved on the stones at the beginning of each chapter and decipher them using the code below. Make sure to keep the letters and numbers in the right order of chapters one through ten!

Once you solve the code, go to www.animaljam.com/redeem or the Play Wild app to redeem your code!*

CODE

Replace	e	j	n	a	8	b
With	A	B	C	D	E	F
Replace	q	k	4	t	f	v
With	G	H	I	J	K	L
Replace	g	5	x	z	l	9
With	M	N	O	P	Q	R
Replace	c	m	h	p	o	u
With	S	T	U	V	W	X
Replace	w	y	s	d	r	1
With	Y	Z	1	2	3	4

*Each code valid for a one-time use.